CatKid

I'm No Fraidy Cat!

Hi! My name is CatKid.

That means I'm one whole-half cat and one whole-half kid. It also means I'm totally cute! Most people have never seen a half-cat, half-kid before. Know why? Because I'm special, that's why!

CatKid

I'm No Fraidy Cat!

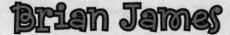

Brian James

illustrated by

Ned Woodman

A
LITTLE APPLE
PAPERBACK

SCHOLASTIC INC.

New York Toronto London Auckland Sydney
Mexico City New Delhi Hong Kong Buenos Aires

ISBN-13: 978-0-439-88854-7
ISBN-10: 0-439-88854-9

Book design by Tim Hall

12 11 10 9 8 7 6 5 4 3 2   7 8 9 10 11 12/0
40

Printed in the U.S.A.
First printing, April 2007

To my faithful cat, Doggie, for all her
inspirational shenanigans!
— B.J.

CatKid

I'm No Fraidy Cat!

Chapter 1:

That Big Scary Noise

I, CatKid, sit right up in my bed when I hear that big scary noise.

"HEY! STOP ALL YOUR RACKET!" I holler at the noise.

Know why?

Because it's late, and I, CatKid, am trying to get some sleep, that's why!

And besides, I'm not scared of noises. My dad says that's because I'm one brave kitten.

Only know what?

I'm not even a kitten anymore, that's what!

I'm a full-grown CatKid!

After I'm done shouting, I don't hear any more spooky noises. Good.

I bet it was only thunder, and thunder isn't as scary as it sounds.

I put my head right back down on my pillow. Then I pull the covers all the way over my head. And finally, it's nice and quiet again.

But just then, I hear a different noise. It's not big or loud. My ears start going all twitchy. That's because I have cat ears, and sometimes they go all twitchy when they start hearing things that are really, really squeaky.

Sometimes it comes in handy to be able to hear squeaky things. I can hear my teacher's squeaky shoes coming before anyone else. So I hardly ever get caught doing stuff I'm not supposed to do, like talking or passing notes.

That's when it's good to hear squeaky noises. Only I can hear squeaky noises

right now. And it's no fun hearing them when I'm trying to get my beauty sleep!

And anyway, I've got a little secret.

See, I'm not afraid of the big noises, but those squeaky noises sometimes scare the pants off me. Like now! Only, my pants don't really come off. I checked. But still, I'm the teeniest, tiniest bit afraid.

I peek a little way out from under the covers.

"Who's there?" I whisper.

Nobody answers.

Maybe all that noise is only the wind.

I try to listen harder.

Listening, listening, listening.

I hear it again!

And then I know for sure that it's not the wind. Know how?

BECAUSE THAT NOISE IS COMING FROM INSIDE THIS HOUSE, THAT'S HOW!

And that makes me one giant bit afraid.

That's because I hear those squeaks again, and they're right above my room. It sounds like someone is creeping back and forth all over the place.

Only I know nobody is up there, because that's the attic. Nobody ever goes in our attic because it's dark and smells funny.

And that's when I, CatKid, know it can only mean one thing. . . .

GHOSTS!

And I do NOT like ghosts!

I make a great big *hissssss,* because if those

are ghosts up there, I want those ghosts to get lost!

Only my hissing doesn't work, because just then those mean ghosty things make another giant big noise! Maybe they are trying to get into my room.

I leap straight up into the air and fall, right off my bed! Lucky for me, cats always land on their feet.

I run right out of my room.

I run into my mom and dad's room.

I jump onto the bed and make a leaping dive under the covers!

That wakes up my mom and dad.

"What's the matter, sweetie?" my mom asks. She sounds tired, but this is important. If this place is all haunted and stuff, then they shouldn't be sleeping, anyway! I'm doing them a favor, so there!

I peek out from under the covers and make a *shhhhhh* sound.

I whisper to her about how I'm hiding from those ghosts.

"What ghosts, pumpkin?" my dad asks.

"Those ghosts that are making all those noises in my room, that's what ghosts!" I tell him.

But my dad says he didn't hear any noises.

Then my mom says she didn't hear any noises, either.

And then I say, "Maybe that's because you don't have cat ears like me."

"Maybe it was just thunder," my mom says.

"Nope, I checked," I tell her.

"Then maybe it was the wind," my dad says.

"Nope! I checked that, too!" I tell him.

Then they say it's only my imagination playing tricks on me.

"Nope," I say. "My imagination would never do that. Me and my imagination are friends."

My mom takes a deep breath.

"Well, I guess you can sleep here tonight," she says. Then she scratches me behind my ears, because I like that scratching-behind-my-ears thingy.

Only it doesn't make me feel any better, because I'm too busy keeping a lookout in case those ghosts try to get into this room, too!

They'd better beware of me, CatKid, because I'm one tough watchcat! And there's no way I'm gonna let them catch me sleeping on the job.

Chapter 2:

Classroom Catnap

"CatKid? CatKid wake up!"

That shouting makes me shoot my head up off my desk. I look all around, and my tail goes all bushy, just like a squirrel's tail. That's what happens when I get startled.

The other kids in my class go giggly and stuff, even my best friend, Maddie.

My teacher, Mrs. Sparrow, is standing in front of me. She doesn't look too happy.

Usually she's just about the nicest teacher in the whole entire second grade,

but not if you've been falling asleep in class.

"That's the second time you've fallen asleep today," she says. Only she didn't even have to say that, because I know how many times I've fallen asleep.

I counted.

And anyway, it's three times, not two.

"I'm sorry," I mumble, even though it's not my fault.

It's the fault of those stupid ghosts!

I had to stay up all night guarding my house and keeping my mom and dad safe.

And anyway, I can't help it if I fall asleep sometimes. That's what cats do even when they aren't haunted all night. It's just easier for cats to sleep during the day. That's why they call it a *catnap*.

Plus, my desk is next to the window. It's a fact that the sun makes a kitty snoozy. And afternoon sun is the best sun for sleeping.

"Are you feeling okay?" Mrs. Sparrow asks.

I look at her and smile real big because that question is a silly question. I always feel better after a nap!

"I feel *cat*-tastic!" I say.

Mrs. Sparrow leans in real close to me.

My nose goes all sniffy. Yum! I can smell the tuna Mrs. Sparrow had for lunch. And that tuna makes me think about fish sticks, because those fishes on a stick are my favorite treats, that's why!

Mrs. Sparrow has to tap me on the shoulder to get my attention because I'm too busy thinking about fish.

"You seem especially distracted today," Mrs. Sparrow says quietly to me. "Is everything okay?" she asks.

I scratch my head thinking about that question.

That's one tough question.

Because when you believe that ghosts are haunting your room, everything is NOT okay.

But there's NO WAY I'm going to tell her about those ghosts. Not in a hundred million years!

If I tell her about what happened last night, even if I whisper it super quiet, then everybody in my class will think I'm a big fat fraidy cat.

"Everything is A-OK!" I say. Then I

smile my whiskers real wide so she'll believe me.

I look around to make sure I fooled everyone. And then I wipe my forehead and take a deep breath because it looks like it worked.

That's what I, CatKid, call a close one!

"Okay, if you say so," Mrs. Sparrow says, "but if you keep falling asleep, I'll have to send you down to the nurse's office."

"No problem," I tell her. "I promise not to fall asleep ever again for the rest of the whole day." And that's an easy promise because there is only a little bit of the day left, anyway.

"Maybe you should send her back to *kitten*-garten!" Billy says. He's always making fun of me. That's because Billy is the meanest boy in the whole wide world. Plus, he's stinky. And to make it worse, he sits at the desk right behind me.

I turn my tail around.

Billy starts making goofy faces. Then he says that only babies take naps and that's why I belong in kindergarten.

That's when I yell at him, "QUIET YOUR FACE!" Because I, CatKid, am *not* a kitten!

"That's enough," Mrs. Sparrow says.

She looks really, really, super mad, too.

I know I'm not supposed to yell in class, but sometimes I just can't help it. That Billy makes me so mad that my voice comes out loud all by itself!

I make a frown.

"Sorry," I whisper.

Then I sit my tail down in my seat.

But as soon as Mrs. Sparrow turns

around, I stick my tongue out at that Billy the Bully!

But then you know what?

He pulls my tail, that's what!

I turn right around in my chair and make a growly sound at him. And even though my mom says I'm not allowed to hiss at anybody, I'm still gonna hiss at Billy if he pulls my tail one more time!

Then he whispers something about getting his stupid dog to chase me.

But it doesn't work, because I, CatKid, am not listening to him anymore. That's what my dad calls "being the bigger person." But I changed it. I call it "being the bigger cat."

Besides, I'm not afraid of his dumb old dog, anyway! I'm not afraid of anything! Except maybe . . . ghosts.

Mrs. Sparrow starts teaching us more spelling.

Spelling makes me s-l-e-e-p-y.

But I made a promise, so I tell myself not to fall asleep.

That doesn't mean I can't rest my eyes, though. Resting my eyes isn't the same as sleeping, so that's not really breaking my promise.

So I put my head down on my desk again and close my eyes.

Chapter 3:

No Such Thing

That night, I don't want to go to bed. Not in my room, anyway.

"Can't I sleep downstairs tonight?" I ask my parents. "I could build a tent out of the sofa cushions. It would be like camping."

"You know the rule about school nights," my dad says.

Then I make a face, because the rule is that I have to sleep in my room. But that rule never said anything about having to sleep in a haunted room.

"Maybe I could sleep in your room," I say, "just for tonight."

Then my mom reminds me that I already slept there last night. "And besides," she says, "that's why you have your own bed, so you don't have to sleep in ours."

Then I, CatKid, have an idea.

"How about this," I say, "I sleep in your room, but I'll sleep on the floor so you won't even know I'm there." That seems fair to me.

"Is this because of those noises you heard?" my dad asks.

I nod my head up and down.

My dad sure is one smart cookie.

"Come with me, I have something to show you," he says. Then he holds out his hand. I take it, and he leads me to the library room.

He's up to something. I can tell because he has a sneaky smile on his face. He looks up and down the shelves. Then he yells, "Ah-ha!" and pulls a book off the top shelf.

I add all of those things up, and it equals one thing. My dad *must* be up to something!

That book is all dusty and makes my whiskers twitch. Then it makes me sneezy. And I'm just about to hate that book until I read the title.

It's called *There's No Such Thing As Ghosts.* I have never even heard of that book. It sounds like a pretty good book to me.

My dad says it was his when he was a kid

like me. That means the book must be really old.

He reads the book with me. It says that there aren't any ghosts. It says that what most people think are ghosts are really something else, like the wind or a funny light.

When we get to the end, I'm not even afraid of ghosts anymore.

"That's the best book ever!" I tell my dad.

"See, I told you there's nothing to be afraid of," he says. And now I believe him when he says there are no such things as ghosts, because if it's in a book, it has to be true!

But then something makes me scratch my head.

"Hmmm, I wonder what those noises are in my room if they aren't ghosts," I say.

My cat ears and cat sniffing tell me *something* is going on in this house. But what? I've just got to find out. It's a cat thing.

"Uh-oh," my dad says.

"Uh-oh, what?" I ask.

"Uh-oh, you have a curious look on your face," he says. Then he tells me the story about cats and curiosity for about the gazillionth time.

I know all about those silly kitties that get too curious. They go sniffing around in things that get them in trouble. But I don't even have to worry about that, because the book says there are no ghosts. That means there's nothing that will get me in trouble. And so I don't have to be afraid of being curious about those sounds above my room.

Plus, being curious will help me find out the truth.

So I rush upstairs and get ready for bed.

I can't even wait to start snooping around!

I brush my teeth and run into my room. I jump on my bed and pull the covers up. Then I wait. I'm ready for any strange noises or funny smells this time.

They don't start until after everyone is asleep and the whole house is quiet. That's when I hear that scratchy squeaky sound.

I try really hard to figure out what it is.

My dad's book has a list of things that people think are ghosts. I go through the whole list. Only my ghosts don't sound like any of those things.

In fact, they still sound a lot like ghosts to me.

And I can smell them, too.

They don't smell like the wind or a

spooky light. They smell like old leaves, and that is exactly how I, CatKid, think ghosts would smell.

That does it!

I run into my parents' room.

I wake my dad up right away. "Dad wake up! I hear them again!"

He yawns real big. Then he reminds me about the book.

"Yeah, I'm not so sure that dumb old book is true," I tell him.

I make him come in my room to check, but the ghosts are all quiet again.

Not a single squeak.

"I don't see anything, sweetie," he says.

I say, "Well, of course not, they're invisible."

"Well I don't *hear* anything, either," he says.

I take a deep breath. "That's what makes them sneaky, Dad. Everyone knows ghosts are sneaky."

"Well, they're gone now. And it's time to get some sleep." And then he tucks me in and leaves my room.

But I don't sleep even one wink.

I stay awake under the covers waiting for the squeaks to come back.

Chapter 4:

Top Secret!

The next day after school, I, CatKid, keep looking out of the family room window. That's my favorite spot. All cats have one. I even keep my favorite blanket there for when I want to snooze.

I'm not napping now, though.

I'm waiting for Maddie, my best friend in the whole wide world. She's coming over to my house. We have very, very, very, very important things to talk about.

My mom says that looking out the window won't make Maddie get here any faster, but I'm not so sure that's true. So

I keep looking out the window anyway, just in case.

I keep tapping my foot, too. My mom says that doesn't help either, but I do it anyway. Finally, I can't take it anymore. I hate waiting. "Why isn't she here yet?" I ask my parents.

My dad says that I have ants in my pants. Only that doesn't make any sense. Know why?

Because there are no ants in my pants, that's why!

I checked.

I found zero ants!

That means he is wrong and I tell him he shouldn't say things that are fibs.

"It's just an expression, kitten," he says.

"Yeah, only know what? I'M NOT A KITTEN, THAT'S WHAT!" I holler. He's my dad, so he should know I'm a full-grown CatKid.

"Sorry, sweetie," he says.

I don't yell anything at him this time, because that name sweetie is a good name to be called.

My mom calls out my name from the kitchen. I spring up from the sofa and run to the kitchen door.

"Do you want me to make some special treats for you and Maddie?" she asks me.

Special treats are my favorite!

"Um, can you make us some fishes on a stick?" I ask because I just LOVE fish. And fish on a stick is even better.

"I'm not so sure Maddie likes fish sticks," my mom says to me.

And I say, "Oh yeah." I forgot that fish on a stick makes Maddie hold her nose and go P.U.!

"How about I make some cookies?" my mom says.

My mom is one smart lady, because cookies are almost just as good as fish sticks. And plus, that Maddie really, *really* likes cookies.

"Do you want to help me?" she asks.

"Yeah, only you know I can't," I tell her.

"Why not?"

"Because," I shout, super excited, "I hear Maddie's mom's car!"

Like I said, my cat ears have very good hearing.

I cat-sneak over to the front door. Then I open it real slow like one cool cat, and Maddie is standing there.

She gets all giggly. She always gets giggly when she comes over.

"I couldn't wait to get here!" she says, and that makes me smile.

I help her take off her coat and her shoes.

There's a rule in my house about not wearing shoes. I call that *being a tidy cat.*

My mom says I should let Maddie catch her breath. "You're making the poor girl dizzy," she says.

I ask Maddie if she is dizzy, and Maddie shakes her head no.

"See, she's not even dizzy, so there!" I say to my mom. "For a mom, you say some silly things sometimes."

My mom rolls her eyes. That's what

moms do when they've been proven wrong.

Then I whisper to Maddie real quiet. "We're going up to my room for a secret meeting."

I grab her hand and pull her up the steps and into my room. We shut the door real tight because we have TOP SECRET stuff to talk about!

The TOP SECRET stuff is about ghosts!

I've just got to get somebody to believe me!

That's why I asked Maddie to come over to my house. She's my best friend, so she has to believe me. *And* she's not allowed to think I'm a fraidy cat. Those are the rules of being best friends.

"Maddie, true or false? Are there even such things as ghosts?" I ask her.

"That's easy!" Maddie says. "False. Everyone knows that."

"Yeah, but you know what?" I say. "I'm not sure, because how come I heard all those noises last night and the last night before that one, too?"

"What noises?" Maddie asks.

Oops! I forgot that I forgot to tell her about them.

So I start to make a loud sound like a *boom* and then a scratchy sound, too. It's kind of like the sound our teacher, Mrs. Sparrow, makes when she writes too fast on the chalkboard.

"What noises are those? I never heard any noises like that in my whole life," Maddie says. Then she raises her eyebrows real big the way she does whenever she thinks I'm fibbing.

I do a frown and make a huff.

"Those are the exact noises that I'm trying to tell you about!" Then I point up at the ceiling because that's where the noises come from.

"I don't hear anything," she says.

"They only make noises when it's dark out," I tell her.

Maddie starts to look a little bit afraid. Then she asks, "Do you think maybe ghosts are real?"

"I don't know, but I have to find out!" I tell her. Then I make a fist because those ghosts really make me mad by coming here to scare me.

I want to find out everything about them. I want to know where they come from and how they got so sneaky. Also, I want to know why they are in *my* room, and what makes them smell so funny! Because those ghosts have my curiosity running wild, that's why!

"I'll help you," Maddie says.

That makes my tail go waggy. Because I, CatKid, sure am lucky to have the bestest best friend there is!

"Let's think of a plan," she says.

Then the both of us go all quiet and scratch our heads because that's what you do when you try to think.

Think, think, think, think, think!

Only I, CatKid, can't think of anything.

"Are you thinking?" I ask Maddie.

"I'm thinking," Maddie says to me.

Then we go back to being quiet and thinking. But after a long time of think-ing, my head starts to hurt.

"I couldn't think of anything," I say.

"Me, neither," Maddie says.

But just then, I do think of something! But it has nothing at all to do with ghosts or noises, because what I'm thinking about are the cookies. I can smell them all over the place!

"Maybe if we go eat a whole bunch of cookies, it will help our brains think up a plan," I say.

"*That's* good thinking," Maddie says.

Chapter 5:

Spying!

I, CatKid, am in what my mom calls a *"very big rush!"*

I hear the noisy school bus coming down my street.

I grab my lunch box as I rush out the door. I wouldn't want to forget it because it has my favorite lunch in it. Fish sticks!

Yummy!

"Bye," my mom says.

Then I say, "Bye right back," as the bus pulls up.

When I get on the bus, I sit my tail down right next to Maddie. And I know exactly

where she is, too, because she is standing up and shouting my name.

When the bus starts driving, Maddie tells me a secret that I didn't even know. Last night, she asked her big sister if there was any such thing as ghosts, and know what her sister said? Her sister said that there was too such a thing. And Maddie's sister knows EVERYTHING!

"And besides that," Maddie tells me, "she showed me a book called *True Ghost Stories!*"

Then Maddie pulls that book out of her backpack.

I open up my mouth and make a *gulp* sound!

I don't know which book to believe — the one my dad showed me, or this one. "Which one do you think is right?" I ask Maddie.

"I don't know, but this one has PROOF that ghosts are real!" she says.

The book my dad showed me didn't really *prove* that ghosts aren't real. It just proved that some people made mistakes about ghosts. "Then your book must be true," I say. "And that book my dad showed me must be one big fat fib!"

Then I make a growl. I'm not so happy because I was tricked. I heard those noises all last night. Only I didn't believe they were one hundred percent real, so I wasn't one hundred percent afraid.

Now I know they are real and that makes me mad! I make my hand into a fist. Now I've got to figure out a whole plan to get rid of them spooky ghosts and fast!

That's when Billy looks over the back of our seat.

He was spying on us!

I cover up the book real quick.

Billy is the last person that I, CatKid, want knowing about me and ghosts.

"What's that?" he asks, pointing to the book that I'm trying to hide.

"None of your beeswax," I say.

"Yeah," Maddie agrees. Then she folds her arms and lifts her head up high. "These ghost stories are none of your beeswax!"

My eyes go all big.

"You just told him," I whisper to Maddie. "It was supposed to be TOP SECRET, remember?"

She covers her mouth real quick. "Ooops, sorry."

Sometimes I'm not sure Maddie gets the whole point of this TOP SECRET thing.

"Those stories aren't true. They're fakes!" Billy says. "You're fraidy cats if you believe them."

"These stories are *so* true!" Maddie says. She holds the book right up in his face. "See! *True Ghost Stories!*"

"Fakes." Billy says.

Then we try not to listen to him. My mom calls that "*ignoring him.*" But it's hard to ignore him when he keeps making scary ghost noises and stuff.

"Only fraidy cats believe in ghosts," Billy says.

"Yeah, only guess what?" I tell him, "I'm not a fraidy cat! And anyway, you have to sit down!"

"Who's going to make me?" Billy says.

Then the bus driver says, "Billy, take your seat."

I stick out my tongue when he sits down and Maddie starts laughing. But I don't laugh, because I, CatKid, still have very serious ghost troubles and absolutely zero plans for how to get rid of them!

Chapter 6:

Big Fat Mouth

I raise my hand up really high and wag my tail around in the air so that Mrs. Sparrow will call on me.

She is making a list on the board of all the different kinds of stories we can name. Then, each kid in my class can pick a kind of story to write for weekend homework.

I'm waving my hand real fast because I know a whole bunch of stories.

First, she calls on Maddie.

Maddie tells her, "Stories about unicorns." Then she claps her hands and giggles because unicorns make Maddie go silly.

"Those are called *fantasy* stories," Mrs. Sparrow tells us. Then she writes the word *fantasy* on the board.

I give Maddie the thumbs up when she looks at me because that answer was a good answer. I just love those unicorn stories.

Mrs. Sparrow calls on Bradley second.

Bradley is a smarty-pants. He names a gazillion different kinds of stories.

"Biographies and autobiographies and

history," he says. Mrs. Sparrow can't even write them all down as fast as he says them.

I roll my eyes at Bradley because naming all those kinds of stories is getting on my nerves. I haven't even had my turn yet.

Then finally Mrs. Sparrow calls on me.

"Fairy tale stories!" I shout. "Especially that one where Little Red Riding Hood teaches that dog a lesson."

"That was a wolf, Dumb Ears!" that bossy girl Shelly says to me.

"Same thing, Dumb Face!" I say.

Mrs. Sparrow says for both of us to stop calling each other names even though Shelly started it. Shelly's always calling me Dumb Ears.

I was just sticking up for myself.

Billy raises his hand next.

When Mrs. Sparrow calls on him, he leans over his desk. That way he is talking right into my ear when he answers, "Spooky stories."

My ears perk up when he says that. It makes me remember the book Maddie had on the bus. Then I get a little shiver because that book is one spooky book. Plus it's not even a story, because it's a fact. There's a reason it's called *True Ghost Stories*.

I think spooky stories can be true because I have a spooky story *happening* in my very own room.

Mrs. Sparrow writes *spooky stories* on the board.

I, CatKid, do NOT like spooky stories.

"I don't even think spooky stories are spooky," Shelly says right at Billy. "I don't believe them. Nobody believes them!"

"Yeah, nobody believes them," the whole class says. That makes Billy look like he's the only one in the world who thinks spooky stories have any spook in them.

I don't say anything. Because I'm trying to be one cool cat, that's why. Being a cool cat means not letting anybody know

that secretly I'm a little bit scared of those stories.

But being a cool cat doesn't even matter once Billy opens his big fat mouth again.

"CatKid believes them!" he says. "She said so on the bus today."

The whole class goes quiet. Then everybody is looking at me instead of him. I don't even know what to do with myself.

So I turn my tail right around.

"Did not!" I shout at Billy.

"Did too!" he shouts back.

"DID NOT!"

"DID TOO. You said spooky stories were true," he says.

"I didn't say spooky stories were true," I say. "I said that *ghost* stories were true! And you would, too, if you had a ghost living right above your bed like I do, so there!"

But then I put my hands right over  my mouth, because that part about the ghosts slipped, that's why! And now it's not TOP SECRET anymore. The whole entire universe knows that I, CatKid, believe in ghosts!

The whole class makes *ooooohhhhhs* and *aaaahhhhhs*. They start pointing at me because nobody in the second grade is supposed to believe in ghosts.

That's a rule!

Ghosts are for babies.

Then my whole entire face turns red, and it's all Billy's fault.

He tricked me!

That's no fair!

"CatKid's afraid of ghosts!" he teases. Some of the kids in my class start laughing when he chants, "CatKid's a fraidy cat!"

"Am not!"

"Are too!"

And I'm just about to yell again when Mrs. Sparrow comes over to our desks.

She folds her arms. That means she's really mad. "I want both of you to stop acting up," she says.

If we don't stop, she'll write both of our names on the board.

Getting your name on the board means you're in trouble. So we both close our mouths real tight.

When it's time to pick what kind of

story we want to write, I don't even care. That's because I, CatKid, have bigger fish to fry, that's why. Only that's not as good as it sounds, because it has nothing to do with fish. It just means I have a lot of work to do. That's just what my dad calls an "*expression.*"

I, CatKid, have to figure out a way to prove that I'm no fraidy cat. And the only way to do that is to catch that squeaky ghost who is living in my house!

That's my most important weekend homework!

chapter 7:

Recess Success

My whole lunch is ruined!

It was supposed to be the best lunch ever, but this ghost business is spoiling it. That's because Shelly's in the cafeteria, too, and she keeps teasing me about ghosts.

"I'm not listening to you!" I say to Shelly. Then I take out my fishes on a stick.

None of my friends think I'm a fraidy cat. They say that anyone who can eat fish on a stick has to be pretty brave. That means I'm the bravest kid in the whole wide world, because I could eat fish sticks all the time, that's why!

Then I see Shelly hold her nose. "Fish are gross!"

"Yeah, well you're gross!" I say. Then I smile because that showed her!

But then I see other kids holding their noses, too. And my cat ears can hear Shelly whispering mean things.

She tells everyone about what happened in class. She even tells some kids at the third graders' table! "Cats shouldn't be

allowed in school, especially fraidy ones!" she says.

And that is why I, CatKid, can't even enjoy eating my fishes on a stick. Sometimes it's not easy being one whole-half cat.

But I know there's something going on at my house. My cat ears and cat nose tell me so. I have to come up with a foolproof ghost-catching plan. That way everyone will know how brave I am and that being half-cat is the best.

When recess starts, I march my tail right over to the monkey bars. I leap right up to the top. That's because I find those monkey bars the absolute best place for planning!

But I'm not good at thinking up plans all by myself. The best plans come when I have friends to help me think.

So I smile my whiskers real wide when I see Maddie coming over with Kendra and Preston. That's because those are my three bestest friends in the whole world. Plus, they are all really good at coming up with plans.

"Hi, CatKid!" they say.

"Hi, right back," I say.

I tell them they are just in time. Then I take a piece of paper and a blue marker out of my pocket. Now I am ready to make my Blue Prints.

"Okay, what's first?" Preston asks.

"That's easy," I say. "The first part is to get somebody to sleep over at my house. That way it won't be as scary."

So I write that down.

1. *Somebody should sleep over at my house.*

"So, who's it going to be?" I ask.

"I can't," Preston says. "I'm going to my grandparents this weekend. Plus, I'm a boy."

That's true. No boys are allowed to sleep over at my house. It's a rule.

"Um, I can't, either," Kendra says. She looks around. "Don't tell anyone, but I'm sort of afraid of ghosts, too," she whispers.

"That's okay," I tell her. Then I promise to keep it a secret, especially from Billy.

"I'll sleep over," Maddie says, "but I have to ask my mom first."

That part is easy. She just has to say, "Please, please, pretty please with sugar on top!" when she asks. That's the best way to get Maddie's parents to say yes to anything.

Then I write down the number two. Only I have no idea what to write next.

"I know!" Kendra says. "Number two should be baby powder!" But I don't write that down because I don't even know what she's talking about.

"Ghosts are invisible, so you need to pour baby powder on them so you can see them," she says. "I saw that on TV once."

And I write that right down, because that baby powder is a good idea.

2. *Baby powder*

That will be easy to get, too, because Maddie has a baby brother, and he's always full of that powder.

"Cookies! That should be number three," Maddie says.

"What are those for?" I ask.

"For bait, silly!" she says.

And guess what? Using bait is one good idea. So I write that down, too.

3. Cookies

I'll ask my mom to make a whole big plate full of them.

Then Preston scratches his head. "You need something to set off the trap."

"I know! I know!" I shout. "STRING!" And I get all excited because that string stuff is the best! I could just play with that string for hours and hours and hours!

"I can get some," Maddie says.

4. String

Now we have all the ingredients for a trap.

That's when I give the Blue Prints to Kendra, because Kendra can draw the best of all of us.

We watch as she draws a picture of my room. Then she draws where the baby powder goes and where the cookies go. Then she makes a whole bunch of scribblely lines for the string.

"Tie one end of the string to the

cookies, and one end to the cup of baby powder," Kendra explains. "When the ghost takes 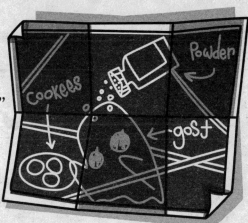 the cookie, the baby powder will get all over it. Then you'll be able to see the ghost, so you can catch it."

"That's perfect!" I say. I'm so curious about that ghost, I can't even wait to get my paws on that noisy thing. I've got to show it who's boss-cat around my room!

Right then, Maddie pokes me in the side and points. I see that bossy girl Shelly and her snotty friend Olivia walking over to us.

I'll show them how brave I am.

I leap off the top of those monkey bars and land right on my feet. I always land

on my feet,
because
it's a
cat-fact
that I,
CatKid,
am one
good jumper.

Shelly jumps back a little.
Then she makes a face like she smelled
something rotten. She always makes that
face when I do something only a half cat
can do.

"Look, it's the fraidy cat!" Shelly says.

"Yeah, only this proves I'm no fraidy

cat!" I shout, waving the piece of paper at her face.

"What's that?" asks that girl Olivia, who is in the other second-grade class.

"Duh. Blue Prints for a trap!" I say, and I roll my eyes because that's pretty easy to tell with all the blue marker all over it. I don't think they teach anything in that other second-grade class!

"That paper doesn't prove anything," Shelly says.

"Yeah, only know what?" I say. "If I'm setting a trap to *catch* a ghost, it proves I'm not *afraid* of ghosts!"

Then she rolls her eyes at me and says, "But you still *believe* in ghosts, and that's just as silly."

"Of course I do, that's because I can smell them up in my attic. And my nose never lies," I say. Then I hold my head up real high, because there's nothing wrong with believing in the truth.

"You smell them? That's yucky," Olivia says.

"Smells fishy to me," Shelly says, "but maybe that's just your breath!"

I stick out my tongue and say, "That's because I'm a whole-half cat, and I like fish. Get over it!"

"Let's go," Olivia says to Shelly. "I think I'm allergic to cats."

"That's okay, because we're allergic to meanies!" Kendra shouts. Then we all pretend to go all sneezy and stuff as they walk away.

I'll show them! Once that ghost is caught, they won't be able to make fun of me, so there!

Chapter 8:

Ready, Set, Trap!

"Time to begin Special Mission: Ghost Trap!" I announce when Maddie tosses her sleeping bag on my bed. That's the name we came up with for catching ghosts.

I made it up all by myself!

Except for the "Special Mission" part.

Maddie came up with that.

I make sure the door to my room is shut tight. I don't want those ghosts to spy on us when we set the trap. Plus, I don't want my mom to see, either, because she doesn't like things like traps.

She has another name for traps. She calls them "*one giant mess*" instead.

I pull out the Blue Prints from under my pillow. I had put them there for safe-keeping. That's where I put everything that I want to keep safe.

The first order of business is making sure we have all the ingredients.

"Did you bring everything?" I ask Maddie.

"Yep! It's all right here in my sleeping bag," she says.

"Goody!" I shout.

I stare my eyes real wide when Maddie takes the string out of her sleeping bag. And I can't even wait to get my paws on that string.

I just love that stringy stuff!

I'm just about to pick up the ball of string and chase it all around my room when Maddie stops me.

"Maybe I better be in charge of the string," Maddie says.

"Yeah, but maybe I could just play with

it for one quick little second," I say.

Then Maddie shakes her head and giggles. "You know you can't control

your cat half around string," she says.

"I guess you're right," I say. "The trap is more important than playing with string."

Then I make my face all serious, too. That's because ghost catching is hard work. I'll have lots of time to play with string after we trap the ghost!

We follow the Blue Prints exactly!

First, Maddie stretches that string all around my bed. Then in front of the windows. Then under my desk. That ghost could come from anywhere, so she even stretches it from wall to wall so that there is no place that ghost can go without running into the string.

Next, we put the baby powder stuff in a paper cup. We tie the string around it and set the cup on a shelf over where the cookies will go.

We're all finished with the string when there's a knocking sound on my door.

"Who is it?" I ask.

"Me," my dad says.

"Me, who?" I ask, because maybe it's really a ghost trying to be all sneaky.

"Me, your father."

Maddie says I should ask him what the secret password is, just to make sure. That's a good idea.

"What's the secret password?" I ask.

He answers, "I brought you cookies."

That's not the password at all.

The secret password is *abracadabra*.

Only know what?

I don't even care, because I need those cookies, that's what!

I open the door only a tiny bit because I don't want my dad to see the trap. He might tell us to clean it up before my mom sees it, and that would ruin everything.

I whisper to my dad that he can set those cookies right down outside the door.

Then he asks me why he can't come into my room.

"Because, this meeting is TOP SECRET!" I whisper-shout to him.

"Oh, okay," he says and puts down the

cookies. I wipe my forehead and make a whistle sound, because that was one close call.

Now the plan is all set.

As long as me and Maddie can keep ourselves from eating all the cookies before it's time for bed.

Chapter 9:

Bump in the Night!

When I, CatKid, open my eyes, I don't hear any squeaky noises. The only noises I hear are the snores coming from Maddie's sleeping bag.

I think maybe that snoring is keeping my ghost away.

So I make a *shhhhh* sound!

And guess what?

It works, that's what!

Maddie rolls over and that snoring goes away. And now that I'm awake, I can wait for the ghost and catch it when it comes.

I sniff with my nose, but I can't smell any ghosts. I only smell cookies.

But then I have an idea.

My idea is to check to make sure the ghost didn't already sneak in. So I climb out of my bed and tippy-toe over to the door. That's where those cookies are.

It's a good thing that I can see in the dark, too, because that string is EVERYWHERE! I have to duck under it here, and climb over it there. Plus, I have to try really, really hard not to pull on it or the trap will go off.

Finally, I make it through.

All of the cookies are still on the plate. I count them. One, two, three, four, five, six, seven, eight, nine, ten. That means no ghosts came in.

And I'm just about to go back to my bed when I my nose goes all sniffy. That's because those cookies still smell so good.

And know what?

Seven cookies is probably enough to catch a ghost, that's what!

So I, CatKid, grab three of the cookies!

Then I start eating them all up. And my nose wasn't even wrong at all, because those cookies are delicious!

I'm just about to tippy-toe back to my bed when I see a piece of string hanging out of place. It's just dangling there.

That makes me stop right in my tracks.

I know I promised not to play with the string, but maybe I should just put it back where it belongs.

But before I put it back in place, it probably wouldn't hurt if I just batted at it once.

So I do.

Only it starts to swing back and forth.

And then I know I have to stop it before Maddie wakes up and catches me, so I give it a tiny tug.

But guess what?

That tug makes the whole trap go off! My eyes watch the string whiz past my bed, and over my desk, in front of the window, and above my head. And then that baby powder stuff dumps down all over me and I scream.

I see Maddie sit right up in her sleeping bag. Then she points.

"GHOSTS!"

Maddie yells so loud I don't even know where to turn my tail.

That's when me and Maddie run right out of my bedroom and all the way down the hall, straight into my parents' room.

My mom and my dad sit right up in their bed. Then we yell at them. We tell them that thing about ghosts being in my room.

"This time, it's really for real! Maddie saw one!" I tell them.

"Why are you all white?" my mom asks. "What's all over you?"

I look at Maddie and Maddie looks at me and both of us are covered in that stupid baby powder.

"It's part of the trap," I say. But I'm not even friends with that trap anymore because that trap didn't work one little bit.

"What trap?" my mom asks.

"That's not important," I say. "The important thing is that my room is one hundred percent HAUNTED!"

That's when my mom rolls her eyes and looks at my dad. That's what she does when it's my dad's turn to come and look. But I don't even care whose turn it is, because this time Maddie saw the ghost.

This time they'll see I'm not making things up.

I pull him out of bed. I don't want those ghosts getting away!

"Come on!" I hurry him up. I've got to know the truth once and for all. I can't take another minute of being curious!

"Okay, let's check." And that's when my dad gets out of the bed. Me and Maddie stay behind him, because my dad is one brave dad, that's why.

He's not even afraid of any ghosts. But I think that's only because he doesn't know about that *True Ghost Stories* book.

When we get to my room, my dad opens the door. I see his eyes go all big and everything. "Do you see the ghost?" I ask him.

"Worse," he says, and me and Maddie make a giant *gulp*, because maybe there is a whole family of ghosts in there. But then my dad says, "I see a mess. You'd better clean it up before your mother sees it."

"I know that, but is there a ghost? Is there? Is there?"

"I'll go have a look," my dad says.

Me and Maddie don't even think about going into that room. It's safer to wait in the hallway.

My dad disappears in my room.

I feel my legs shake.

I look at Maddie, and her legs are shaking, too.

And then we both cover our eyes, because if that ghost jumps out, we don't want to see it!

Chapter 10:

Gotcha!

My dad is in there a long time.

I try to listen, but everything is really quiet.

What if that ghost Maddie saw is hiding, and it's going to pounce on my dad?

I just start thinking maybe the ghost got my dad, but then I hear someone coming out.

I hold my breath.

I peek through my fingers.

Then I let my breath out when I see it's only my dad coming out.

"Did you catch it? Did you? Did you?" I ask my dad.

"No," my dad says. "But you know what? I did hear the squeaky noise."

DOUBLE GULP!

Because if my dad heard it, it can't be my imagination.

I knew there was something up there! My cat senses are never wrong!

"It's a ghost, right?" I ask.

My dad shakes his head.

"Is it a monster?" Maddie asks.

I didn't even think of that! And now both of us are officially full-blown fraidy cats because we can't stop shaking, that's why!

"No, no," my dad says, "not monsters. Don't worry, girls."

Then I take a deep breath. If it's not monsters or ghosts, then I take back that part about being full-blown fraidy cats.

Now my curiosity is running wild! Scary or not, I've got to know what's making all those noises!

I try to put all the clues together. The

clues are: 1) lots of squeaky sounds, 2) a few loud sounds, and 3) a funny smell that smells a little bit like leaves.

With those clues, it could be ANYTHING!

It's one big mystery to me!

We follow my dad over to the attic door.

He opens the door and we stand back.

"How about we wait right here," I say, because even if there are no ghosts up there, I can still smell something coming from that attic, and it smells hungry. I hope it doesn't like the taste of cats!

"Okay," my dad says and goes up the creaky steps to the attic.

Me and Maddie wait at the bottom of the stairs.

Even Maddie can tell the attic smells funny.

So we hold our noses. Then we make funny faces that mean that attic is one stinky place.

"Ah-ha!" my dad shouts. That's what he says whenever he is right about something. So that means there isn't a ghost at all. "Girls, come and take a look," he says.

I look at that Maddie and she looks at me.

We shrug our shoulders, because my dad said that *ah-ha*, and so there's nothing to be scared of.

Then when we walk up those creaky steps, I make a growly sound. That's because I, CatKid, cannot even wait to get my paws on whatever was making all  that racket!

I'm going to chase it all over the place!

I sneak up next to my dad. I look to see where he's looking. Then I take a long stare in the corner and open my eyes wide, because I don't even believe my whiskers when I see what's been living in our house.

Chapter 11:

True Ghost Story!

I, CatKid, cannot even wait for school to start. That's because our class is going to read our weekend homework stories today.

I spent all day yesterday working on my story.

It's perfect!

"Mrs. Sparrow, can we read our stories now?" I ask as soon as I walk into the classroom.

"As soon as we say the Pledge and sing our morning classroom song," she says.

"Oh, yeah," I say.

Usually those are two of my favorite

things. But today I forgot all about them because I'm so excited.

It takes forever for everybody to sit at their desks.

Then it takes double forever to say the Pledge.

And then I'm the only one who sings the words really fast. It takes triple forever to finish the song because Mrs. Sparrow makes us start all over when someone doesn't sing with the class.

But then FINALLY Mrs. Sparrow says

it's time to share our stories with the class.

I raise up my arm really high.

But then that Billy the Bully tugs on my tail, so I have to put my arm down and turn around.

"What's your story about, chasing mice?" he teases.

"No," I say, "that would be an *adventure* story, and my story is a spooky, true, mystery kind of story."

"Ohhhh," he says, "I'm real scared." Then he pretends to be shivery.

"Yeah, well my story is going to scare your pants off, EVEN YOUR UNDER-PANTS!" I tell him. Then I giggle a little bit because that *underpants* word is a funny word.

Mrs. Sparrow calls on Kendra. And I don't even mind, because Kendra always has the best stories.

This time her story is about a fish that

can fly. And
that's what I
mean when I
say her stories
are the best,
because I love
fish stories.

I give her the thumbs up when she's done reading. "That was a great story," I whisper, "even if nobody got to eat that fish."

"Thanks," Kendra says.

But then I forget to raise my hand, and Mrs. Sparrow calls on Bradley. His story is about a boring old robot that meets a dinosaur in space.

Only everybody knows there are no dinosaurs anymore, so I'm not crazy about that story.

Then the next turn is the best turn. That's because Mrs. Sparrow calls my name.

I jump right out of my seat and run up to the front of the room.

"Mrs. Sparrow, can we turn off some of the lights?" I ask. "My story is a spooky story, and turning the lights off is what I call 'setting the mood.'"

Mrs. Sparrow smiles a little bit and says, "Okay."

Some of the kids in my class get a little spooked in the dark. I can tell as soon as the lights go off. Like Billy. I can see he's nervous that he can't see now. I'm not. My cat eyes see perfectly fine in the dark.

"My story is a true story," I start.

"But you said it was a spooky story, so it can't be true," Shelly says.

"Yeah, only know what?" I say. "It's my turn, so you have to be quiet please. Thank you."

Shelly rolls her eyes.

Then I start again. I read the title out

loud first, "*How I Caught a Ghost* by me, CatKid."

I hear some of the kids in my class giggle when I read the part about how there were ghosts living above my bed. But they stop real quick when I start making scary noises like the ones I heard.

"And nobody else could hear them," I whisper. "Nobody believed me, either, but I stayed on the case! I, CatKid, like to find out the truth about things. And the truth was, those ghosts were on a sneaky haunt. If I didn't have cat ears, they may have never been caught."

Then the class makes *oooohhhs* and *aaaahhhs*, and I can tell they are starting to believe me. Billy's eyes go all big. I can tell even Shelly isn't so sure spooky stories are fakes anymore.

"That's when me and Maddie set a trap to catch the ghosts," I read. "Only the

ghosts were too clever. They never took the bait."

"How did you catch them?" Kendra calls out.

I look up at Kendra. "I'm getting to that part next," I say.

I start reading my story again. "My dad snuck up the stairs to the attic. I covered my eyes and listened to the creaky stairs, step-by-step. Then, all was quiet. I held my breath. I thought maybe my dad got pounced on by those ghosts. Then . . . all of a sudden . . . out of nowhere . . . MY DAD SHOUTS AT THE TOP OF HIS LUNGS!"

Every one in my class makes a *gulp*.

I can hear them whispering. I see Shelly cover her eyes. I see Billy cover his ears. Then I smile because they are both scared silly!

And then I get to the scariest part.

"My dad," I read, "was face-to-face with a real . . . live . . . hungry . . . pack of . . . SQUIRRELS!"

And when I scream that part about squirrels, everybody gasps and giggles.

Then I smile my whiskers, because I, CatKid, scared them. It was one spooky story!

I tell the rest of the story about how those squirrels are the most adorable, cutest, fuzzy, little squirrels ever. "And the loud sounds I heard were just them knocking things over in the attic, because it's a fact that squirrels are clumsier than cats."

"The end," I say, and everybody claps.

And not even one person calls me a fraidy cat, either. That's because catching squirrels is brave work, that's why!

Even Billy says, "I'm sorry I called you a fraidy cat."

"And I'm sorry right back for scaring you silly," I say.

Then I smile all proud. Because I, CatKid, proved to the whole class that I'm no fraidy cat. And I used my cat senses to do it. That's why I like being one whole-half cat, and why I like being me.